This book belongs to:

_____

My pet's names are:

_____

My favorite animals are:

_____

Mimi and Maty to the Rescue!

Book 2

Sadie the Sheep
Disappears Without a Peep!

Written by Brooke Smith
Illustrated by Alli Arnold

Better World Kids Books
New York

Sky Pony Press
New York

For Kelly and Mimi and our life on Rock Springs.
And for Dad, who taught me how to "just bee."

— Brooke

For the kids and the animals that keep me inspired.

— Alli

Sky Pony Press books may be purchased in bulk at special discounts for sales promotion, corporate gifts, fund-raising, or educational purposes. Special editions can also be created to specifications. For details, contact the Special Sales Department, Sky Pony Press, 307 West 36th Street, 11th Floor, New York, NY 10018 or info@skyhorsepublishing.com.

Sky Pony® is a registered trademark of Skyhorse Publishing, Inc.®, a Delaware corporation.

Visit our website at www.skyponypress.com.

10 9 8 7 6 5 4 3 2 1

Manufactured in China, November 2013
This product conforms to CPSIA 2008

Library of Congress Cataloging-in-Publication Data is available on file.

ISBN: 978-1-62636-344-1

CHAPTER ONE

It's spring break, and Maty and I are going to visit Aunt Bee's farm!

Super - Amazing

Maty's my three-legged rescue dog. She's a super amazing dog and my very best friend.

Aunt Bee is my beekeeping, honey-making aunt. Her and my uncle Al's farm is one of Maty's and my favorite places in the whole wide world.

Uncle Al
←

Aunt Bee
→

Of course bees live there.

But so do horses,

ducks,

10

chickens,

cows,

and sheep!

And one special sheep named Sadie is why Maty and I are *so* excited to go. Because Sadie is (drum roll please) . . .

. . . having a baby!

A fuzzy, wuzzy, super fluffy, cute-as-a-button baby sheep!

Sadie is my favorite animal at the farm. She looks just like a panda.

Sweet smile →

← Baby on Board

Looks like a panda!

And since Maty and I are official animal rescuers and *love* helping animals, we get to help take care of Sadie's baby!

So . . . yesterday, I got on the computer and read everything I could about baby sheep.

Maty and I have never taken care of a newborn anything, so I wanted to make sure we found out everything we could, because official animal rescuers need to be prepared.

I got out my rescue notebook and wrote a bunch of stuff down . . .

Baby Sheep Facts:

1. There are 1,000,000,000 sheep in the world! So when Sadie's baby is born, there will be one billion and ONE.

2. Lambs can walk one minute after they're born... so watch out!

3. Mama sheep can have 1, 2 or 3 babies and maybe even quadruples! ← (whew!)

4. A group of sheep is called a "flock" and the flock keeps everyone safe, sort of like a family, I guess.

5. Sheep make a sound called a BLEAT. A baby knows what their mama's bleat sounds like so they can always find her.

6. Newborn baby sheep can be bottle-fed... ☆ YAY!!! ☆

Aunt Bee even said I could name the baby. So, I wrote down a couple of ideas, to get a head start.

Some ideas if it's a girl:

- Lulu
- Lizzi
- Sarah
- Daisy
  (my favorite flower)
- Definitely NOT Vicky

Or if it's a boy:

- Sam
- Monty (←Maty likes this one)
- Simon
- Willy
- Definitely NOT Dicky!

The other awesome part of our visit is that Aunt Bee got me my very own beekeeper suit!

Yep, I'm going to be a junior beekeeper. Maty didn't get one because bees kind of freak her out. So Mom bought her a bee costume instead. (She especially likes the antennas.)

Plus, I'll use some of the honey to make Maty her favorite cinnamon honey dog treats. She loves them.

Honey Dog Treats

Ingredients:
1 + ¼ cup Whole Wheat Flour
½ cup milk
1 Teaspoon cinnamon
2 Tablespoons honey

Directions:
Preheat oven to 350°F. Combine all ingredients in a bowl, mix well. Knead dough into ball and roll onto a floured surface ¼" thick. Cut with cookie cutter of your choice. Place on greased cookie sheet and bake for 15 min. or until browned at the edges. Cool, then refrigerate.

I really want to show Aunt Bee how excited I am about being a beekeeper. So while I was on the computer, I looked up a bunch of bee facts too . . .

Bee Facts:

1. Honey bees have been making honey fo_ 150 million years !!!!!!!!!!!!!!!!!!!!! wou_

2. They're the only insect that makes food for humans.

3. Bees have ④ wings, ⑥ legs and ⑤ hai_ eyes. Yep, they have hair on their eye_

4. Bees use the sun for a compass.

5. The buzzing of a bee comes from it_ wings flapping super fast: 11,000 stro_ a minut_

6. Honey bees never sleep. (No wonder they're called busy bees.

7. The largest bee in the world is th_ size of a Tootsie Roll (1.5").

8. The smallest bee in the world is the size of a freckle (1/16").

9. Bees can count to four.

10. There's one queen bee per hive and she lays 1,000 eggs a day.

11. Honey bees can fly up to 15 miles per hour!

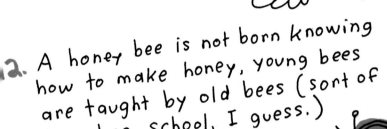

FAST!

12. A honey bee is not born knowing how to make honey, young bees are taught by old bees (sort of like bee school, I guess.)

13. A bee's brain is oval!

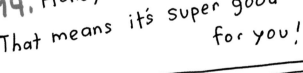

14. Honey is a SUPERFOOD
That means it's super good for you!

Tootsie

Wow. Bees are

Amazzzzzing!!!…

Since Mom and Dad can't come to the farm until tomorrow, Aunt Bee said she'd pick us up this afternoon. Sadie's baby might pop out any minute and she doesn't want us to miss a thing.

I put my rescue notebook in my backpack along with a bunch of other stuff we might need. I was helping Maty try on her new doggy day pack . . .

. . . when all of a sudden she ran to the front window and started barking!

Sure enough, Aunt Bee was pulling up in the driveway. I kissed Mom goodbye, ran out the door, and jumped into Aunt Bee's pick-up truck.

Wow. Spring break with Maty, Sadie, and her fuzzy wuzzy baby. Am I one lucky animal-loving girl or what?

CHAPTER TWO

We were almost to the farm when Aunt Bee said we had to make a quick stop at the Farmer's Market.

That's where Aunt Bee sells the stuff she makes out of all her honey, like lotion, candles, and jars and jars of BEE HAPPY HONEY (her specialty).

Aunt Bee thinks that honey has super powers. She loves it and she loves all her busy bees. (After finding out how cool bees are, I have to say, so do I.)

I asked Aunt Bee who was watching her booth when she came to pick up Maty and me. She said her friend Holly and Holly's little boy, Henry, were standing in for her.

Henry's a great kid. Whenever Maty and I visit the farm, Henry always comes over and we have a blast—he's up for anything!

We climb trees, get in mud-fights, play Frisbee, and hang out with all the animals.

Henry loves animals (I told you he's a great kid)!

As soon as we got to the booth, Henry came running over to Maty and me.

We told him about Sadie and how she's going to have her baby any minute now. He asked his mom if he could come with us . . . and of course she said yes.

Then I overheard Holly tell Aunt Bee about a lady and her daughter who want to visit Aunt Bee's workshop to see how honey's made. I guess she wants to meet the bees.

The girl said she was a friend of mine and Maty's, so Holly told her that she'd have Aunt Bee call them. *Hmmm,* I thought. *It'll be fun to show a buddy around the farm.*

Henry said the girl had "tall hair" that sort of looked like a beehive . . .

. . . and that her name starts with a "V."

"A V!" I stopped dead in my tracks. "Don't tell me her name is Vicky . . . as in the one-and-only ICKY VICKY?" I shouted.

"Yep, that's it," Henry said, not knowing the awfulness of what he just said.

"Well, just so everybody knows, Icky Vicky is *not* my friend!" I shouted. "She's mean and nasty, and if she told you she's my friend she's lying!"

Aunt Bee looked over at me and said what she always says when I'm not being especially nice:

"Remember, Mimi, you can catch more flies with honey than with vinegar."

I know, how weird is that? And what does vinegar have to do with me?

I guess what Aunt Bee means is that I should try to be a sweetheart, not a sourpuss—then things work out better.

I told her that she has *no* idea how icky Miss Vicky can be and how mean she is to Maty. But that didn't faze Aunt Bee one bit. She just smiled and said we better get going. Sadie's waiting for us.

She's right. There's no way Icky Vicky's going to rain on this parade. Henry, Maty, and I jumped back into Aunt Bee's truck and we were off.

Don't worry, Sadie and soon-to-be baby. Help is on the way!

CHAPTER THREE

As we drove up the lane to the farmhouse, we saw Uncle Al on his tractor.

He'd just been down checking on Sadie. No baby yet, but he said she's super excited to see us.

Henry, Maty, and I couldn't wait another minute! We jumped out of the truck and headed straight for the sheep pasture.

Sadie was standing in the middle of the field. She had a huge smile on her face and was wearing a red bandana—one just like Maty's.

They looked like twins!

We ran over and I gave her a huge hug (her belly's so big I could barely get my arms around her), and Maty gave her tons of kisses.

Sadie lay down in the grass to rest, so we all lay down right next to her and stared up at the sky.

We took turns trying to guess what the clouds looked like (one of my all-time favorite farm games, by the way).

Henry saw a hamburger, an ice cream cone, and a pretzel.

(I think he's getting hungry.)

Maty thought every cloud looked like a dog bone.

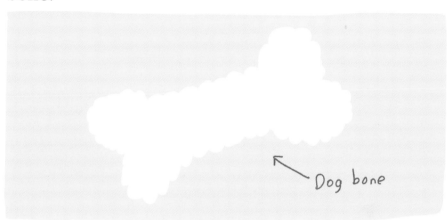

Dog bone

And, of course, I kept seeing baby sheep.

Awwwww.
Baby sheep!!!

Uncle Al came down to see if we wanted to help with some chores while Sadie rested. He said it would give us a chance to visit some of the other animals.

"Of course we would!" I said.

He also wanted Maty and me to keep our eyes out for any animals that might need our help. He knows we're official animal rescuers and are ready to jump into action whenever the tiniest critter needs a helping hand (or paw!).

I took out my notebook and wrote down our list of chores:

Farm TO-DO list:

- Feed the chickens ... fill feed bowl to the top.
- Treat the horses and donkey to yummy apples.......
- Muck-out the stables.
- Brush Snow's (the pony's) white fur. (She's been rolling in dirt again.)
- ~~Chen~~ Check on Sadie to make sure she's still resting.

* Also, keep an eye out for any animal (big or small) that might need our help.

First, we went the barn to feed Coco the chicken and all her feathered friends.

Coco thinks she's a movie star (of the chicken world, of course). She's fluffy and fancy and super glamorous. Coco loves attention and always wants to be pampered.

Next, we grabbed a couple of apples from the apple bag and gave one to Snow . . .

. . . and another to Dino, the donkey.

Snow and Dino are very best friends. Uncle Al calls them the lovebirds of the farm because they're never apart and they nuzzle each other constantly.

While Snow and Dino were crunching away on their apples, Maty suddenly ran over to the apple tree next to the barn and started to bark and bark . . . really loudly.

A bird's nest had fallen out of the tree and was lying on the ground and Maty had spied it! Do I have the greatest rescue dog or what?

We grabbed a ladder from the barn, climbed up the tree, and put the nest back on its branch.

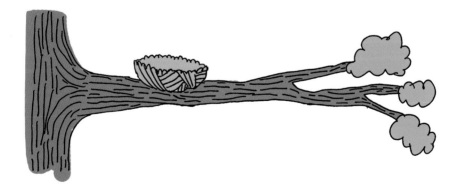

Then we spread birdseed all around to welcome the little birdies back—to let them know everything was A-OK.

When I looked over at Henry, I noticed that he was eating a bunch of birdseed.

He must really be getting hungry.

I decided it was probably time to head back to the house for dinner. On the way, we stopped by the sheep pasture to check on Sadie. She was still resting and seemed really comfy. I kissed her on the head and told her we'd see her in the morning.

We got back to the house just in time. Aunt Bee was pulling out a pan of mac-n-cheese from the oven. We piled our plates high (and Maty's kibble bowl, too) and sat down to tell Aunt Bee and Uncle Al all about our day.

After dinner, Aunt Bee said we could sleep in the teepee out back if we wanted. (Who wouldn't want to sleep in a tepee?) We brought out all our stuff and made it super cozy.

I wish I could sleep in a tepee every night. You can listen to the owls, look at the stars, and pretend you live in an adventure book.

I told Henry and Maty that we better get some sleep—I have a feeling tomorrow's going to be a big day.

I shut my eyes and tried counting sheep . . . lots and lots of baby sheep.

And I'm pretty sure Maty was counting dog treats, because when I looked over, she had a smile on her face a mile wide.

Boy, do I love my dog or what.

CHAPTER FOUR

I was right in the middle of an amazing dream—all the baby sheep I'd been counting were now wearing party hats and singing happy birthday—

HAPPY BIRTHDAY TO EWE, Happy birthday to ewe...

—when all of a sudden Maty started barking, right in my ear.

I woke up and couldn't believe it was already morning. I climbed out of my sleeping bag and peeked outside the tepee to see what was going on.

The second I opened the flap, Maty darted out full speed ahead!

I told Henry to grab my backpack. It had my rescue notebook and tons of important stuff in it. (An official animal rescuer is always prepared.)

We took off after Maty, who was headed straight toward the sheep pasture. As we got closer, I heard another dog barking.

Sure enough, it was Mack, the Border Collie from next door (and Maty's major puppy crush).

Mack belongs to Mr. Francis. He's the sheep guy that Aunt Bee got Sadie and the rest of her flock from.

Mr. Francis loves sheep. He even looks like one.

Mack was busy barking and herding the sheep away from the fence and now Maty was right beside him.

Finally, I saw what was going on. Part of the fence was knocked down, and Mack was trying to keep the sheep from escaping!

YIKES!

Fence post down!

I told Henry to run over and push the fence post back up. Then, I called Maty and asked her to dig (which she loves to do) and I piled the mound of dirt all around the post to keep it standing up.

Phew. We did it. We fixed the fence and all the sheep were now safe and sound in their pasture. Not bad for an early morning rescue, if I do say so myself.

But Maty didn't seem happy at all. She kept barking and barking. I looked around for Sadie to give her a good morning kiss, but couldn't find her smiling face anywhere.

Wait a minute! I bet that's what Maty's trying to tell us:

She probably got out when the fence fell over. Now Sadie is wandering around somewhere, ready to have her baby. Or maybe she's already had it!

I suddenly felt super sad. Maty came running over and gave me tons of kisses. I hugged her and said I was so proud of her for letting us know that Sadie had run away.

As soon as I looked at Maty's smiling face, I knew this was no time to sit around feeling sorry for myself.

Like all good animal rescuers, we needed to act—and act fast!

act fast

First things first . . . we have to get Mack back home. I'm sure Mr. Francis is worried about him and we don't need a lost dog on our hands, too.

And while we're there, I bet he can help us find Sadie. He knows everything about sheep. If I'm going to rescue a sheep, I need to think like a sheep.

Sadie, my dear, have no fear . . . Mimi and Maty are here!

CHAPTER FIVE

Mr. Francis came rushing out of his house
when he saw the four of us coming down his lane.

He'd been calling Mack all morning and was getting really worried. I guess Mack never runs off.

I told him that Mack had done an amazing job herding Aunt Bee's sheep so they didn't escape through the broken fence. The only problem was that one super special sheep did escape . . .

. . . Miss Sadie!

Mr. Francis knew that Sadie was pregnant, so he felt horrible for us and asked if there was anything he could do. I told him that Maty and I are official animal rescuers, so we're used to this sort of thing. But we could sure use his help.

"Of course," he said. "I'll do anything I can to help find Sadie."

We all went inside and Mr. Francis made me and Henry some hot cocoa with a bunch of marshmallows on top.

And he gave two big bowls of kibble and gravy to Maty and Mack.

I took out my notebook and started writing stuff down:

Notes to me:

- Sadie is missing. (!!!!!)

- Maty heard Finn, the Border Collie (yes, Maty's puppy-crush) barking crazy-like.

- We ran down to the sheep pasture FULL SPEED AHEAD (I didn't even have time to change out of my PJ's) and Sadie was GONE!

- Now we're at Mr. Francis' house (Aunt Bee's neighbor) having yummy hot cocoa trying to figure out where Sadie ran off to.

I asked Mr. Francis if he could tell us everything he knows about sheep—you never know what fact might save the day.

Mr. Francis' Sheep Facts:

1. Sheep have excellent hearing! That's a great thing because that means Sadie can hear us when we're calling her name.

2. Sheep get scared by loud noises. This isn't so great because we don't want Sadie to be freaked out.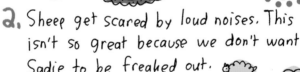

3. Sheep like to eat tons of grass (even though it makes them burp). This could be a good thing because Sadie might stay in one place munching on grass.

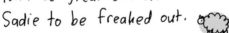

All the sheep facts sounded fine and dandy, but I asked Mr. Francis why Sadie would wander off? I thought flocks stayed together to keep each other safe?

He said that's usually what happens, but sometimes sheep need to be alone. They need a little privacy.

Like when a mama sheep is about to have a baby, or . . .

"WHAT?"

"Did you say that sometimes sheep go off by themselves when they're having a baby?" I shouted so loudly that Maty and Mack jumped under the table.

Mr. Francis said he's heard of that happening. Sometimes a mama sheep just needs to be by herself—away from all the hustle and bustle of the flock.

Well, that's it! At least we know why Sadie ran off. I hurried and wrote down the latest clues:

Latest Clues:

- Sadie ran off to find a cozy, comfy spot to have her baby.

- She wanted to be away from the other sheep so they wouldn't bug her.

- Sadie could be having the baby RIGHT NOW!!!!!

- We better find her PRONTO to make sure that she and the baby are A-OK.

We needed to get back to the farm and tell Aunt Bee and Uncle Al what was going on. The farm's so big that there are tons of places where Sadie could be hiding.

(That's great when you're playing hide-and-seek, but not so great when you're looking for a lost sheep.)

Mr. Francis said
he'd drive us back to the
farmhouse ASAP. I grabbed a
handful of marshmallows for
the road and we headed out
the door.

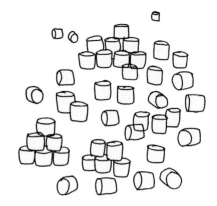

I could tell Maty was
excited to spend a little more
time with Mack—nothing like
puppy love to turn Maty's
frown upside down.

Now, let's find Sadie!

CHAPTER SIX

We jumped out of Mr. Francis's truck and thanked him for all his help. Maty gave Mack a big kiss goodbye and we ran straight into the house to find Aunt Bee and Uncle Al.

Uncle Al was in the kitchen fixing breakfast. We told him everything that had happened and he said he'd head out right away to start looking for Sadie . . . and that we should go get Aunt Bee. She knows every single secret hiding place on the farm.

He told us that Aunt Bee was in her workshop meeting with my friend and her family, to take them on the "honey tour."

"No way!" I shouted. "Not now! This can't be happening!"

I grabbed Henry and Maty and we ran up to the workshop and burst through the door.

Sure enough, there they were: Icky Vicky, Dicky, and their mom.

Just standing there.

The first thing Vicky did was look right at Henry and open her big mean mouth:

"Well, Mimi, who's your miniature friend? I guess you couldn't find someone your own age to play with. No surprise.

"And what on earth are you wearing? FYI, pajamas are for bedtime, in case you didn't get the message."

(This made me steaming mad.)

I could feel my whole body start to shake, but I decided I just had to ignore Icky Vicky. We were right in the middle of one of our biggest rescues ever, and there was no time to waste.

I went over to Aunt Bee to tell her about Sadie . . . when all of a sudden Icky Vicky started to scream (like only Icky Vicky can scream).

EEEEeeee eeeeeee eeeeeee eeeeeee eeeeeK!!!

She'd bumped into a shelf and jars and jars of Aunt Bee's honey had spilled all over her!

Of course, she started freaking out:
"Get this gross, sticky, disgusting, horrible honey off of me *now*!"

Wow! Icky Vicky turned into Sticky Vicky right before our eyes.

Icky Vicky grabbed Dicky and told him to give
her the bandana he'd found so she could wipe all
the honey off. Dicky handed her a red bandana and
I about jumped through the roof (Maty, too)!

It was Sadie's red bandana!

I asked Dicky where he got that red bandana. He said he found it lying on the ground in front of Aunt Bee's house.

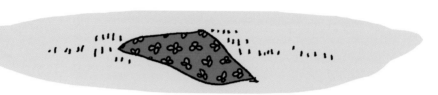

Aunt Bee looked at me and asked what was going on. I told her that Sadie was missing, but not to worry. I think I just figured out where she might be.

But I did have one super important question: Did Uncle Al ever fix the fence around the front porch—the part that was broken right by the stairs?

Aunt Bee said, "No, he still hasn't gotten around to it."

"Hot dog!" I shouted. That was the best news of the day.

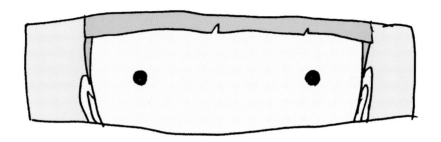

I looked Maty right in the eyes . . .

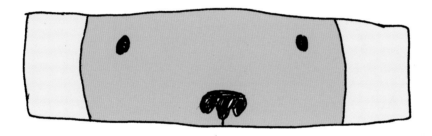

. . . and said three words:

"Hide and Seek."

And that did it! Maty bolted out the door.
Henry, Aunt Bee, and I took off after her. When
we got to the front porch, Henry started to worry
because there was no sign of Maty.

But Henry didn't know what I know . . . that to the right of the stairs is a broken piece of fence that lets you crawl right under the porch.

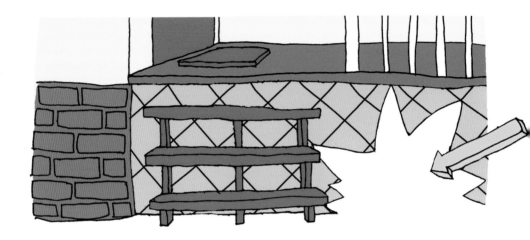

It's always been Maty and my go-to hiding place when we play hide-and-seek.

We all knelt down and looked under the porch, and sure enough . . .

. . . there was Maty, Sadie, and *two* little babies! All safe and sound!

I hugged Aunt Bee, gave Henry a high five, and crawled right under the porch to be with all my fury friends

Finally, Sadie had her babies. And Maty and I had a rescue story we'd never forget.

CHAPTER SEVEN

As soon as Icky Vicky got un-sticky, she and Dicky and their mom walked down to the house to say goodbye. They took a peek at the new babies and said they needed to be on their way.

Then, Aunt Bee did something crazy. She thanked Vicky and Dicky for helping rescue Sadie. She said that if they hadn't come to the farm and found the bandana, we might not have figured out where Sadie was hiding.

Aunt Bee reached into her pocket and took out two of her super cute "bee happy" pins.

She gave one to Dicky and pinned the other on Icky Vicky's T-shirt and told her:

"Remember, Vicky, you can catch more flies with honey than with vinegar"

Here we go again...

Good try, I thought to myself. I know Aunt Bee loves her sweet-vs.-sourpuss saying, but she has no idea that she's talking to the biggest sourpuss of all time.

But then something amazing happened . . .

. . . Icky, Sticky Vicky looked up at Aunt Bee and *smiled*!

Yep, you heard it. Icky Vicky smiled at Aunt Bee and gave her a huge hug.

Wow, maybe honey does have super powers after all. Or, maybe Maty and I just have the best aunt in the whole wide world.

CHAPTER EIGHT

We finally got Sadie and the babies settled in the barn. Maty and I took turns feeding the little lambs so Sadie could rest. She was one tired mama sheep.

83

Aunt Bee asked us if we'd thought of any names yet. I told her I'd written some down in my notebook, but now I think I have a better idea.

"How about Hide and Seek?" I asked. "That way we can always remember the adventure we had when they were born."

Introducing...

Hide + Seek

Aunt Bee loved it!

When Henry's mom picked him up, he told her all about rescuing Sadie. Now he wants to help animals every spring break.

I sat down on a big stack of hay and took out my notebook.

It had been an amazing day and I wanted to finish it up with a huge happy ending.

HUGE Happy Ending and Stuff!

- We found Sadie and her TWO little babies!!!

- They were all safe-n-cozy under the front porch, which is Maty's and my favorite hiding spot.

- So we named them HIDE and SEEK! Hide's a gi and Seek's a boy.

Uncle Al came into the barn and said my mom and dad just called and they're on their way.

I can't wait. Mom loves babies and when she sees Hide and Seek's fuzzy little faces, she's going to go nuts.

Aunt Bee said we should all head back up to the house. She wants to make us some of her famous honeycomb frozen yogurt—a big yummy thank-you treat for helping find Sadie.

She and Uncle Al are so proud of us. They think Maty and I are the most awesome animal rescuers around.

After today, I have to say so do I!

Lost or hurt animals have no fear. Mimi and Maty are here!

Mimi has always loved animals. When she was seven years old, she started a rescue notebook so she could keep track of all the animals she's helped: butterflies, birds, and chipmunks . . . even a rainbow trout!

When Mimi was eleven years old, she wanted to help feed the dogs and cats at her local shelter in Bend, Oregon, so she created the website Freekibble.com. Freekibble has now fed over 11 million meals to homeless pets at shelters and rescues across the country.

Maty is now the Humane Society of Central Oregon's goodwill ambassador. She visits schools and groups, teaching people about animal safety and showcasing the many abilities of a disabled dog. Maty is also the first three-legged dog to qualify and compete in two Skyhoundz World Canine Disc Dog Championships. Way to go, Maty!

Mimi and Maty met through their work at the animal shelter and have been special friends ever since. With their big hearts, Mimi and Maty continue to inspire others to help, care for, and love animals.

Maty and her real life puppy crush

About the Author:

Brooke Smith is Mimi's mom. She has always wanted to write a book inspired by Mimi's big heart and all the fun she has helping animals. With this book, Brooke hopes to get other kids excited to help all of the four- and three-legged creatures that need them.

About the Illustrator:

Alli Arnold is never without a pen and paper. Her first illustration was published when she was just seven years old, and she has gone on to illustrate for such clients as the *New York Times* and Bergdorf Goodman. Alli lives in New York City with her little dog, Nino. To see more of Alli's drawings, go to www.alliarnold.com.